GALAXY ZACK

SPACE CAMP

By Ray O'Ryan

Illustrated by Jason Kraft

LITTLE SIMON
New York   London   Toronto   Sydney   New Delhi

LITTLE SIMON
An imprint of Simon & Schuster Children's Publishing Division
1230 Avenue of the Americas, New York, New York 10020
First Little Simon paperback edition May 2016
Copyright © 2016 by Simon & Schuster, Inc.
Also available in a Little Simon hardcover edition.
All rights reserved, including the right of reproduction in whole or in part in any form.
LITTLE SIMON is a registered trademark of Simon & Schuster, Inc., and associated colophon is a trademark of Simon & Schuster, Inc.
For information about special discounts for bulk purchases, please contact Simon & Schuster Special Sales at 1-866-506-1949 or business@simonandschuster.com.
The Simon & Schuster Speakers Bureau can bring authors to your live event. For more information or to book an event contact the Simon & Schuster Speakers Bureau at 1-866-248-3049 or visit our website at www.simonspeakers.com.
Designed by Nick Sciacca
Manufactured in the United States of America 1216 MTN
2 3 4 5 6 7 8 9 10
Library of Congress Cataloging-in-Publication Data
Names: O'Ryan, Ray. | Kraft, Jason (Jason E.) illustrator.
Title: Space camp / by Ray O'Ryan ; illustrated by Jason Kraft.
Description: First edition. | New York : Little Simon, [2016]
Series: Galaxy Zack ; #14 | Summary: Will troublesome cabinmates ruin Zack's summer at space camp on the planet Sylvan?
Identifiers: LCCN 2015035404| ISBN 9781481463010 (hc) | ISBN 9781481463003 (pbk) ISBN 9781481463027 (eBook)
Subjects: | CYAC: Science fiction. | Camps—Fiction. | Interplanetary voyages—Fiction. | Human-alien encounters—Fiction.
BISAC: JUVENILE FICTION / Readers / Chapter Books. | JUVENILE FICTION / Science Fiction. |
JUVENILE FICTION / Action & Adventure / General.
Classification: LCC PZ7.O7843 Sp 2016 | DDC [Fic]—dc23
LC record available at http://lccn.loc.gov/2015035404

CONTENTS

Chapter 1
School's Out!

Zack Nelson had a huge smile on his face as he waited in line for the lunchtime Sprockets Academy space bus. It was super-hot outside, but he didn't mind. Nothing could ruin his mood today. It was the last day of school before summer vacation!

1

Finally, when the bus arrived, all the kids climbed on board.

As Zack made his way to the back of the bus, he overheard kids talking about their summer plans.

"My family is going on vacation to

Cisnos," said Seth Stevens, one of Zack's friends. "My dad got us passes to Lollyland amusement park."

"We are going to Araxie, the water planet," said Sally Zerbin, one of his classmates. "I am going to spend all summer swimming at the beach."

"I am staying on Nebulon," said another boy. "But that is okay because my parents gave me permission to go to the Starcade every day!"

Zack loved playing the games at the Starcade. Normally he would be jealous, but he had exciting summer plans of his own.

When he reached the back of the bus, Zack slipped into a seat next to Drake Taylor. Ever since Zack and his family moved to Nebulon from Earth, Drake had been his best friend.

"Are you ready for Camp Stellar, Zack?" asked Drake.

"Yeah, I can't wait!" said Zack.

They were going to Sylvan, the perfect planet for space camp. The whole world was covered in forests filled with trees of all shapes and sizes.

"We'll spend every day hiking, swimming, and camping. Plus, we'll get to meet kids from all over the galaxy!" Drake said with excitement.

"And I'll get to add Sylvan to my 3-D planet-collector!" said Zack. "I'm excited to make new friends. But the best part is that we get to hang out all summer!"

"Yipee wah-wah!" Drake agreed.

The bus arrived at the cafeteria, and a few minutes later, Zack and Drake were eating their lunches.

"I am a little worried," said Drake. He took a big bite out of his sandwich. "I have not finished packing."

Zack nodded. He twirled a few strands of twisty noods onto his spork. "I haven't even *started* packing!"

Zack's sisters, Cathy and Charlotte, were sitting at the next table.

"You boys are so . . . ," said Charlotte.

". . . unprepared. We are going to . . . ," continued Cathy.

". . . sing and dance at Glee Camp on . . ."

". . . the planet Aria and . . ."

". . . we've been all packed for days!"

Zack shook his head. He loved his sisters, but sometimes they drove him crazy. He had plenty of time to pack for an entire summer vacation in one night.

The rest of the afternoon went

by slowly, until the final bell rang.

Their teacher, Ms. Rudolph, cheered, "I want to thank you for a great school year. And I wish you all a happy and safe summer."

The boys sprang from their seats and raced outside.

"I'll call you when I get home later," Zack said to Drake. Then he hopped onto the Sprockets speedybus to go home and pack. Summer was here!

Chapter 2
Packing Up

That evening, the Nelson family all gathered around their kitchen table. Shelly and Otto, Zack's parents; the twins; and Zack waited for their food.

"Here is your dinner, Master Just Zack," said Ira, the Nelson's Indoor Robotic Assistant. A panel in the

kitchen wall slid open. Out came a big galactic patty and a steaming plate of crispy fritters.

"So, Zack, have you and Drake finished packing for camp?" his mom asked.

Before Zack could answer, the twins
started singing.

"He is not ready . . . ," Charlotte
cooed.

". . . he hasn't started to pack . . . ,"
Cathy crooned.

". . . but we are all set, unlike you, brother Zack!" they sang together in perfect harmony.

"Now, girls, why don't you let your brother answer for himself," said Dad. Then he looked right at Zack. "You all set, Captain?"

"Um, well, not exactly," said Zack.

He popped a crispy fritter into his mouth.

"How much packing have you done?" asked his mom.

"Uh . . . none," Zack replied. "But I'm going to get it all done tonight."

"Don't forget we need to be at the Creston City Spaceport early tomorrow morning," said Mom. "We're meeting your camp counselor there."

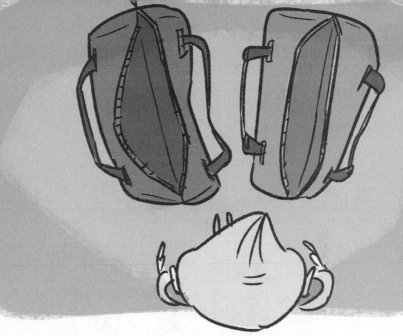

After dinner, Zack took the elevator to his room. Two empty shrink-sacs lay on his floor. Shrink-sacs were invented at Nebulonics, the company that Zack's dad worked for.

They looked like plain duffel bags. But after they were fully packed, they could shrink down to fit into a pocket.

Zack looked at the mountain of things spread out on his floor. He had an all-in-one tent system, perfect for camping out. He had a hover-flashlight that could float and followed him around to light the way on night hikes. He even had a can of Nebulon's strongest bug spray. One small whiff would keep him safe from creepy, crawly, pesky insects from all over the galaxy.

Zack piled socks, sneakers, shirts, shorts, and what seemed like every other piece of clothing he owned on his bed.

"Where do I begin?" Zack asked himself. "I'd better call Drake and see how he's doing."

Zack grabbed his hyperphone and punched in Drake's code. The image that popped up on the screen shocked Zack. It looked like a tornado had hit Drake's room.

"How are we going to fit everything we need into these shrink-sacs?" asked Drake.

"Perhaps I can help," said Ira. "I am programmed to make the best use of any available space."

"Thanks, Ira!" both Zack and Drake cried out.

Ira turned on a vid to show the boys how to properly fold and stack each item so it took up as little space as possible. Zack was amazed at how much these shrink-sacs could hold. With Ira's help, he and Drake were able to pack everything in no time.

"This is my favorite part," said Zack. He pressed a button on the side of the shrink-sacs. The large bags shrunk down to the size of a small wallet. Finally, Zack was all set for camp!

"That was a breeze!" said Zack. "Thanks, Ira!"

"You're welcome, Master Just Zack," said Ira.

"See you tomorrow, Zack!" said Drake.

"Space camp, here we come!" said Zack.

Chapter 3

Journey to Sylvan

That night, Zack dreamed that he was at space camp. He soared above the trees, riding on a flying sled, when a huge bird appeared out of nowhere. It opened its wings ten feet wide.

"Look out!" Zack yelled as he dodged the bird and then fell out of bed.

"Hello, Earth to Zack!" said Mom.

Zack opened his eyes and saw his mom hovering over him.

"Huh? Where am I? What time is it?" asked Zack anxiously. Then he breathed a sigh of relief as his room came into focus.

"Time to get up! You don't want to be late!" exclaimed his mom.

Zack immediately jumped up and hurried to the bathroom. Then he put his shrink-sacs in his pocket and got his backpack.

After eating a quick breakfast, everyone piled into the Nelson family car and drove to the Creston City Spaceport.

The spaceport was busy that day, filled with kids going away to camp. There were so many space cruisers that Zack had a hard time finding his. Then he spotted a hover-sign floating in the air. Bright red letters flashed the words: SYLVAN SHUTTLE TO CAMP STELLAR!

"That's me!" he cried. Zack hugged his mom and dad.

"Have a great summer, Captain!" said Dad.

"Be careful, und have a good time!" said Mom.

"Have fun . . . ," said Cathy. The twins came to see their brother off. They were leaving for Glee Camp the next day.

". . . but not as much fun . . . ," added Charlotte.

". . . as us!" they harmonized.

Zack found Drake waiting by the bus. They waved good-bye to their families and put on their special space camp hats. Tiny planets orbited their heads as the hats lit up with their names.

"Hello, Zack and Drake! I can see from your hats that you boys are going to space camp!" said a tall man. He had thick, craggy skin that looked like tree bark. Green leaves sprung from the top of his head. "I'm Mr. Brod, your camp counselor. Time to go!"

Mr. Brod waved the boys inside as they turned off their names on their hats.

As Zack took his seat, he felt the same thrill he always got whenever he was about to blast off into the galaxy. He loved space travel. He was really excited about exploring a new planet.

Once everyone was settled, the shuttle took off. In a few seconds, they were cruising in space. Zack stared out the window at the stars. He watched as Nebulon got smaller and smaller.

Mr. Brod stood up and walked to the front. "Hello, campers! You are on your way to the best summer ever! At Camp Stellar, the fun is nonstop. You'll play galactic games like capture the glowing electron pod. You'll hang ten in the clouds on airboards, and experience what it's like to float in space. You'll even test your strength in a digi-tug-of-war with a power rope."

"That sounds so grape!" said Drake.

Mr. Brod continued, "We'll also hike in Sylvan's beautiful forests, have a campfire with floating marshmallows,

and go swimming in the lake. Most importantly, though, you are going to make great new friends here."

Zack and Drake smiled at each other. Camp was going to be awesome.

"So sit back, enjoy the flight, and get ready for Camp Stellar!"

Everyone cheered with excitement.

A few hours later, a giant green planet came into view out the shuttle's window.

"Prepare for arrival on Sylvan," announced the pilot.

Zack eagerly looked out the window. His great summer adventure was finally about to begin!

Chapter 4

Welcome to Camp Stellar!

Moments later, the shuttle touched down at the Sylvan Spaceport. Zack, Drake, and all the other kids exited the shuttle in one straight line. They stepped outside to see a thick, lush green forest all around them.

Tall trees waved in the breeze.

Birds sang, and Sylvan mini-monkeys screeched in the distance.

"Okay, campers, follow me," said Mr. Brod.

Zack marveled at how much the counselor blended in with the trees.

Mr. Brod led the
campers onto a
narrow trail in
the woods. As
they hiked down
the path, a tiny bird flew
down and landed on Zack's
arm. It had bright red feathers, orange
wings, and two heads. One head was
blue and the other head was green. It
sang a sweet song, then flew away.

"This is going to be the grapest
summer ever!" said Zack.

After hiking for a few more minutes,
the campers came to a clearing in the

woods. There was a main cabin for large gatherings with several small cabins around it.

"Okay, campers," Mr. Brod said. "It is time to assign you to a cabin." Then he started reading names.

"I hope I can get a top bunk," Zack whispered to Drake.

"Me too," Drake agreed.

Finally their names were called.

WELCOME

MAIN HALL

"Zack, Drake, Connor, and Aiden," Mr. Brod said. "You all are in cabin six, right over there."

All four boys headed into the cabin, and they took off their hats.

"I'm Aiden," said the one about Zack's size. He was covered in fur and looked like a big teddy bear. "I'm from Sylvan."

"I'm Connor, from Zog-13," said the other boy. He was taller than Zack.

Connor had three green arms, three eyes, and tiny caterpillar-like legs. Two long antennae stuck out of his oval-shaped head.

"I'm Zack, from Nebulon. Well, originally from Earth."

"I am Drake, from Nebulon. I guess we should get settled in."

Zack turned a glowing rainbow-colored dial on the cabin's wall. Two sets of bunk beds rose up from the floor. He pulled his shrink-sacs from his pocket. When he pressed the buttons, the bags instantly grew back to their original size.

Zack and Drake tossed their shrink-sacs onto the top bunks.

"Hey!" shouted Connor. "The top bunk is mine."

Zack was shocked. He expected everyone at camp to be friendly.

"Oh, sorry," he said. "Guess I should have asked first." He reached up and pulled his stuff down, sad that his sleeping plans got debunked.

Connor tossed his bags onto the bed and then left the cabin in a huff.

Zack looked over at Drake. "Maybe this summer isn't going to be as grape as I thought," he whispered.

Chapter 5
The Main Cabin

Zack hadn't expected roommate trouble, but he decided to shake it off by unpacking his bags. All of a sudden, the cabin ceiling lit up. It changed into a vid-screen filled with Mr. Brod's face.

"All campers please report to the main cabin," he said.

"Come on," said Drake. "Time to meet the other campers!"

Zack felt excited and nervous at the same time. He looked forward to getting to know the other kids. But after the way Connor treated him, he worried that not everyone would be nice. He sure was glad that Drake was here with him.

Zack and Drake hurried over to the large building in the middle of the camp. They stepped inside and sat down. Connor took a seat in between Drake and Aiden.

Mr. Brod stood at the front of the cabin.

"Let me officially welcome you all to Camp Stellar!" he said. His wooden face broke into a big smile. The leaves on his head stood straight up. "We will all begin and end each day by meeting here. This morpho-cabin will also change into the cafeteria, where you'll eat all your meals."

Zack looked around. He was amazed by all the different kids who were there. He recognized people from some of the planets he had visited. There was girl from Drexel, a huge boy from Plexus, and a pair of twins from Mirer. There were also kids from Cisnos, Juno, Araxie, and Gluco.

"You'll have lots of fun," Mr. Brod continued. "But there are some important rules we all need to follow. First, pick a space buddy for the summer. Always know where your space buddy is. Second, never wander off on your own. Third, lights out at nine p.m. Everyone needs to get a good night's sleep. Fourth, all campers must report for every meal. Finally, hyperphones should stay off at all times. If you need to make a call for any reason, please come to me. Now, take a moment and find your space buddy!"

"Space buddies?" asked Zack.

"Space buddies!" said Drake.

Zack and Drake each lifted one hand with their palms facing out. Then they moved their hands in small circles in front of their faces. This was how Nebulites shook hands.

Zack spotted Connor talking to Aiden.

"You're with me," said Connor.

Aiden's eyes opened wide. He looked around nervously.

"Well, I—"

"Good, then it's settled," declared Connor, interrupting him.

Zack didn't like the way Connor seemed to be pushing Aiden around, but he shrugged it off.

"Okay," said Mr. Brod. "Let's start the day with some exploring! Like I said, remember to stay with your space buddy. Everyone must report back here in one hour."

Drake excitedly jumped up from his seat. "Come on," he said. "Let us go check this place out!"

Chapter 6

Game Time!

Zack and Drake followed a winding trail that started behind their bunk. Flowers that Zack had never seen before grew along the path.

"Look at these," Zack said. He pointed to a batch of tall flowers. They had orange stems that twisted into a spiral like the straws Zack used to drink boingoberry shakes on Nebulon. Every petal on each flower was a different color. "It looks like a rainbow garden!" exclaimed Zack.

The two friends saw a series of curved ridges. The ground rose up like a wave in the ocean. Trees grew from the bottom, top, and sides of each ridge.

"I read about these things," said Drake. "They are the anti-grav ridges of Sylvan. Watch!" Drake ran up the side of the curved ridge—then kept going to the top. Soon, he was completely upside down!

Zack ran up the ridge and joined his friend. "It doesn't even feel like we're upside down," he said. "Everything seems normal."

When the free-time hour was up, Zack and Drake returned to the main cabin.

"Okay, campers! Today we are going to play a game called capture the glowing electron pod," explained Mr. Brod. "First, we'll divide into teams. Each team will have a glowing electron pod placed at their home base on either side of the camp. Every player will be given a power container. The first team to capture the other team's electron pod and bring it to their home base wins!"

"Sounds similar to a game we used to play back on Earth called capture the flag," Zack whispered to Drake. "I was always good at that. I'm a fast runner."

Mr. Brod continued, "If you tag a player on the other team, that player is frozen in place until a teammate tags him. When you're frozen, you won't be able to run after anyone. So it's important to have good offense and defense on both teams."

Teams were based on cabins, so Zack, Drake, Aiden, and Connor were all on the same side. They were playing against the kids from cabin two.

Then Mr. Brod blew his whistle and the game began. Zack looked around but couldn't find Connor. He also didn't see his team's electron pod. A few seconds later Connor appeared.

"I hid our pod," he said.

"Where is it?" asked Zack.

"Don't worry. They'll never find it," Connor said proudly.

"But how can we defend it if we don't know where it is?" Zack asked.

"You just stand right there!" Connor said. "Aiden, Drake, come with me."

Connor ran off to find the other team's pod.

Ugh, who made him boss? Zack thought.

Connor dashed off searching for cabin two's electron pod when a kid from the other team tagged him.

"Ahhh! I'm stuck!" Connor cried out in frustration. He was frozen in midair.

Drake quickly ran up and tagged Connor, unfreezing him.

As soon as he got back down on the ground, Connor ran off to catch the kid that tagged him.

"A thank-you would be nice," Drake called out.

On the other side of the camp, Zack chased away a kid from Plexus. As Zack ran back to his original position, he saw someone dart into a patch of bushes. The kid captured a glowing electron pod and secured it in his power container. Then he bolted toward the cabin two home base.

As soon as the mystery kid ran out
of the bushes, Zack saw who it was. It
was Aiden!

"Oh no! Aiden, stop!" Zack cried.
"You've got the wrong electron pod!

Chapter 7
Trouble in Cabin Six

Aiden raced toward cabin two's base with his power container clutched under his arm. He was so excited to win the game for his team that he didn't hear Zack at all.

Then out of nowhere, two kids from the other team tagged Aiden at the same time. He immediately froze in midair.

"Thanks for finding your own pod for us!" one boy cried as he grabbed the container and ran away. "Now we're going to win!"

A moment later, the final whistle blew and the game was over.

As Aiden's feet touched back on the ground, Connor rushed up to him. "What were you thinking?" Connor shouted. "You stole the wrong pod! You are the worst space buddy ever! I wish I had picked someone else."

"I—I'm sorry. I didn't know it was our pod," said Aiden. He turned and walked away.

"Aiden, don't worry!" Zack called after him. "It's just a game."

But Aiden kept walking, his head hung down. Zack felt bad seeing how hard Connor was on him.

"Aiden will be okay," said Drake. "I am sure he will be feeling better by lunchtime."

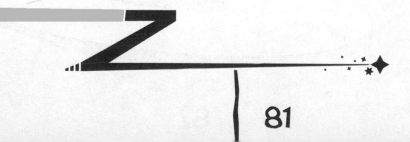

Zack and Drake walked into the main cabin. Mr. Brod punched a code into a keypad. The chairs that had been set up that morning rose into the air.

Slots in the floor slid open. Long tables popped up from below the floor. The chairs floated back

down, and the meeting tent became a cafeteria.

Zack and Drake joined the kitchen line. They filled their trays with food from all over the galaxy. They grabbed Araxie steaks and Plexi potato mash. Zack was happy to see crispy fritters from home.

Once their plates were full, they
went back to their table. They looked
for Aiden, but there was no sign of him
anywhere.

After they ate, Zack and Drake
headed to their cabin. They found
Aiden lying in his bed.

"You're going to miss lunch," said
Zack.

"I'm not hungry," Aiden replied. "I
just want to be alone."

"Don't worry about the game," said
Zack. "We played a game on Earth
called baseball. One time I ran around

the bases backward. Everybody makes mistakes. It's no big deal."

"Yeah, do not let Connor bother you, Aiden," said Drake. "He is just really competitive."

Aiden sat up and looked at Drake. "Thanks, guys. I really thought I was

helping." He sighed. "This is my first time away from home. I really miss my family."

"I know what you mean," said Zack. "When I first moved to Nebulon, I was really homesick. I didn't know anyone. I missed my best friend Bert so much.

Then things got worse because a kid named Seth Stevens picked on me. Things are better now, though. Seth and I are even friends. And of course, I also met Drake."

Aiden smiled.

"I'm happy to have new friends like you and Drake," he said to Zack.

"Me too!" Drake agreed. He pulled out Aiden's hand and taught him how to do the Nebulon handshake. Then all three boys did it at once and started laughing.

Right then, Connor walked into the cabin. "And what's so funny?" he snarled.

"The Nebulon handshake," replied Aiden. "Want to learn it?"

Connor shook his head and rolled his three eyes. His antennae waved back and forth.

"You know, Connor, the real reason we lost is because we didn't work as a team," Zack said. "You wouldn't even tell us the hiding spot!"

Connor stepped back. Zack got the feeling that no one had ever talked to

him this way before. Zack hoped that he would apologize to Aiden. Then they could all be friends.

Instead, Connor said, "I don't have to listen to you," and he stomped away.

Zack looked over at Aiden. His smile had disappeared.

"Don't worry," said Zack. "I have an idea!"

Chapter 8

Campout

The next day, everyone packed up their sleeping tents for an overnight campout in the woods. Mr. Brod led the campers along a winding narrow trail.

Soon, they reached a small clearing. It was lined with curved ridges, like Drake and Zack had seen before.

"These are the famous anti-grav ridges of Sylvan. Space buddies, pick a ridge and set up your tents," Mr. Brod announced. Zack and Drake picked a large curving ridge.

Drake set up his tent at the bottom of the ridge. So Zack walked up along the curved ridge to the top. Zack set up his tent along the top of the ridge, directly opposite Drake.

Once everyone was settled, the campers spent the day hiking and swimming. Later, as the sun began to set, they all gathered around a cosmic campfire. Instead of regular flames, the burning logs gave off tiny shooting stars.

"Does anyone have a good campfire story?" asked Mr. Brod.

Zack, Drake, and Aiden all looked at each other.

Zack spoke up. "I have a story," he said. Then he began: "A long time ago, a creature known as the Sylvan Sticker lived in these woods. This monster had a fur-covered body, sharp pointy teeth,

and long legs and arms shaped like sticks. The Sylvan Sticker didn't like being disturbed, so it would camouflage itself on the ground under the trees. One day, a boy was passing through the forest. Along the way, he found a cute

furry animal asleep in a nest of sticks. The boy knelt down to pet the cute little animal. Then the animal woke up and reared its ugly head. It was the Sylvan Sticker! It stood high above the boy and plucked him into the air."

As Zack was busy telling the story, Aiden and Drake quietly snuck off into the woods. They each picked up a stick.

"That happened many years ago, so people believe the Sylvan Sticker has vanished," Zack said. "But I think it still roams these very woods . . . looking for someone to . . . *scare!*"

At that moment, Drake and Aiden poked Connor with their sticks. Connor shrieked in surprise, and everyone burst out laughing . . . everyone except Connor. He jumped up and ran off into the woods.

Chapter 9

Dinnertime!

Zack felt good about giving Connor a taste of his own medicine. He was sure that Connor would be back any second.

When the laughter died down, Mr. Brod led the campers to a clearing and placed his backpack on the floor. When he pressed a button, the bag opened and food instantly landed in front of each camper.

"These are sylva-nuts," Mr. Brod explained. He handed each camper a round brown object about the size of an Earth softball. "The only place in the galaxy they grow is here on Sylvan. Slip them onto a stick and hold them over the campfire."

"I used to roast hot dogs over a campfire back on Earth," said Zack. Then he placed his sylva-nut onto a stick and spun it over the fire. He took a bite. Zack's eyes lit up. "Wow! Yumzers! This is grape!"

"It is sweeter than the nebu-nuts we have back home," said Drake. "Very tasty."

Zack was surprised by how full he was after just one sylva-nut.

"I have a treat from Earth that I would like to share with everyone," Zack said. He opened up his pack and pulled out the fixings for s'mores. "They are called s'mores. These are a must-have when camping on Earth."

Zack started building and melting s'mores, and he passed them around. Everyone loved them!

Aiden pulled a small bottle from his backpack. "This is syrup made from the bondak tree here on Sylvan," he explained. "One drop makes everything super-sweet."

Zack put a tiny drop on his next s'more. "Yippee wah-wah!" he cried. "My s'more is super-sweet!"

Soon it was time to settle in for the night. Zack walked up the curved ridge. He and Drake were about to go into their tents, when Aiden came running.

"Connor isn't back!" cried Aiden.
"Our tents are right over on the next
ridge. I stuck my head into Connor's
tent to say good night, but he's not
there!"

Chapter 10
Space Buddies

"We have to find him," said Zack. "He's all alone in the dark."

Aiden opened his pack. He pulled out a long clear crystal. "Mr. Brod gave me this Sylvan glo-crystal," he said. "You can use it like a flashlight. Come on!"

Aiden led the way. Zack and Drake followed. After a few minutes, they arrived at Water-Rise Lake. Zack noticed that water from the lake flowed up the side of the mountain. The boys hiked a steep trail next to the up-fall. At the top of the trail, they spotted Connor.

"Hey! I'm so glad we found you, space buddy!" said Aiden. "Are you okay?"

"No, that story was too scary," admitted Connor. "You guys really freaked me out. And you made everyone laugh at me. This camp is my first time being away from home. Now I'm scared *and* embarrassed. How can I go back and face the other campers? They'll all make fun of me."

Zack was shocked. The last thing Zack thought was that Connor was afraid. "Then why were you so mean and bossy to everybody?" asked Zack.

"I thought that if I let anyone know I was scared, they wouldn't like me," said Connor. "So I hid it by acting like I was in charge. I'm sorry, Aiden. I know I wasn't very nice to you."

"And I'm sorry my story scared you so much," said Zack. "It was supposed to be in good fun."

"Yeah, sorry I poked you," said Aiden. Drake nodded in agreement.

"It was kind of funny," said Connor with a chuckle. "I must have jumped three feet when you scared me."

The boys smiled at one another, and they all broke into laughter.

"I am glad we sorted things out!" said Drake.

"Me too! Please come back with us, Connor. Now that we are all friends, we are going to have the best time this summer!" said Zack.

"Yeah, we should get going before Mr. Brod starts to worry," said Aiden.

The boys hiked back to their tents.

"I'm still a little scared," said Connor.

"I have an idea," said Zack. "Why don't we all sleep in my tent?"

"That sounds great!" said Drake.

The four boys walked up the curved ridge and snuggled into Zack's tent for the night.

The next day, everyone returned to the main grounds. After breakfast, Mr. Brod changed the cafeteria back into the meeting room. He read off the list of activities for the day.

First up were races on airboards. These were like surfboards you rode in the air.

"They are made from the same trees that grow on the anti-grav ridges here," Mr. Brod explained. "You can do flips in the air without feeling like you're upside down!"

The boys raced through the course on airboards. They zoomed along, three feet above the ground, as they did all sorts of flips and tricks in the air.

Aiden won the race. Connor lifted all three of his arms and gave his space buddy a three-way high five.

Swimming in the lake was next. Drake was especially excited.

"You know, I used to be afraid of swimming," Drake told the others. "But Zack helped me. Now I love to swim!"

The boys all jumped into the water.

"I miss my family," Zack said as he floated on his back. "But I'm going to miss you guys when camp is over." Zack was glad they were all friends now.

"That's not until the end of summer," said Connor. He ducked

under the
water so only
his antennae
stuck out. Then he
popped back up, making
a big splash. "We have
lots of time to have fun
until then!"

6

"You said it," agreed Zack. Then he shouted, "Last one back to shore is a rotten Sylvan Sticker!"

This was turning out to be a stellar summer!